Dottie and Dots See Animal Spots

Dottie and Dots See Animal Spots

Learning Braille with Dots and Dottie

Kristie Smith, M.Ed, TVI
Illustrated by: Kandice Knorr

iUniverse, Inc.
New York Lincoln Shanghai

Dottie and Dots See Animal Spots
Learning Braille with Dots and Dottie

iUniverse books may be ordered through booksellers or by contacting:

iUniverse
2021 Pine Lake Road, Suite 100
Lincoln, NE 68512
www.iuniverse.com
1-800-Authors (1-800-288-4677)

ISBN: 978-0-595-47130-0 (pbk)
ISBN: 978-0-595-91411-1 (ebk)

Printed in the United States of America

Hi. My name is Dottie and this is my best friend, Dots. Dots and I are both Braille cells.
A Braille cell is what holds Braille letters and words together in one place. There are six dots inside of each of us. Dots 1, 2, 3 are on the left side and dots 4, 5, and 6 are on the right.
I'm very proud of my dots and would love for you to look at them and see where they live.
Dot 1 lives on the left side at the top of the cell. Dot 2 lives in the middle on the left side while dot 3 lives on the left side at the bottom of the cell. Dot 4 lives on the right side at the top of the cell. Dot 5 lives in the middle on the right side while dot 6 lives on the right side at the bottom of the cell.
Ever since my friends and I have learned Braille, we see the Braille appearing everywhere.

Braille is so much fun to learn. Letter a sits on dot 1 and letter b sits on dots 1 and 2, but letter c is made from dots 1 and 4.

Look at the Braille alphabet below and see if you can read the Braille while we go on a fun trip to the zoo.

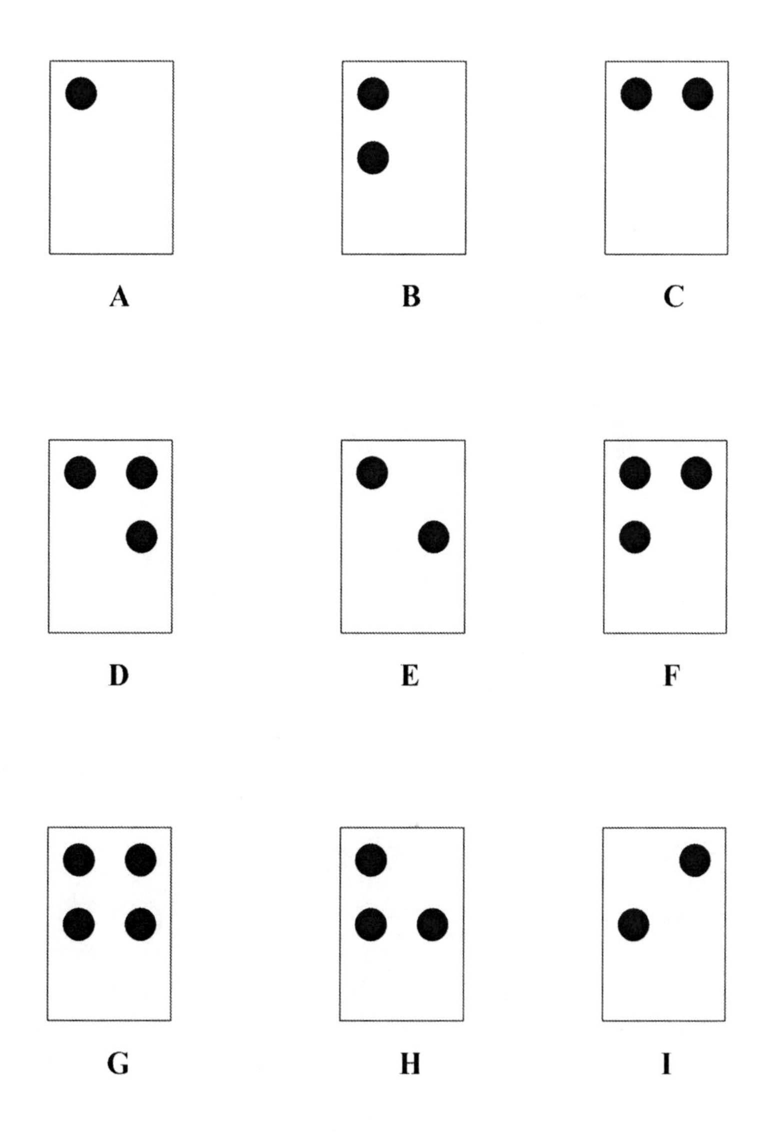
A
B
C
D
E
F
G
H
I

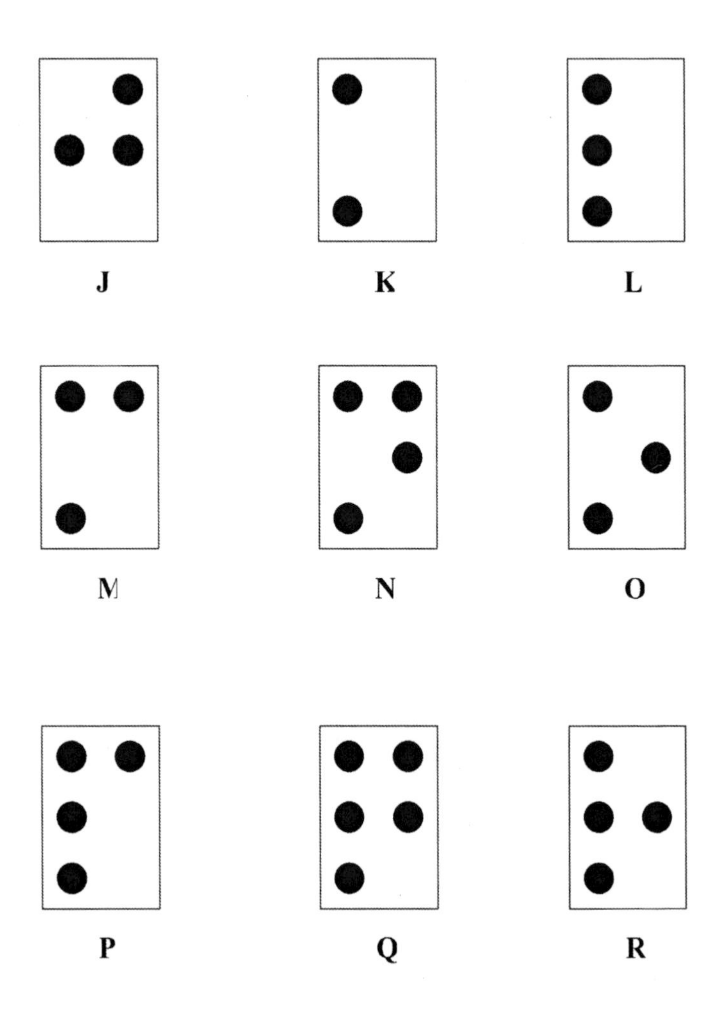
J
K
L
M
N
O
P
Q
R

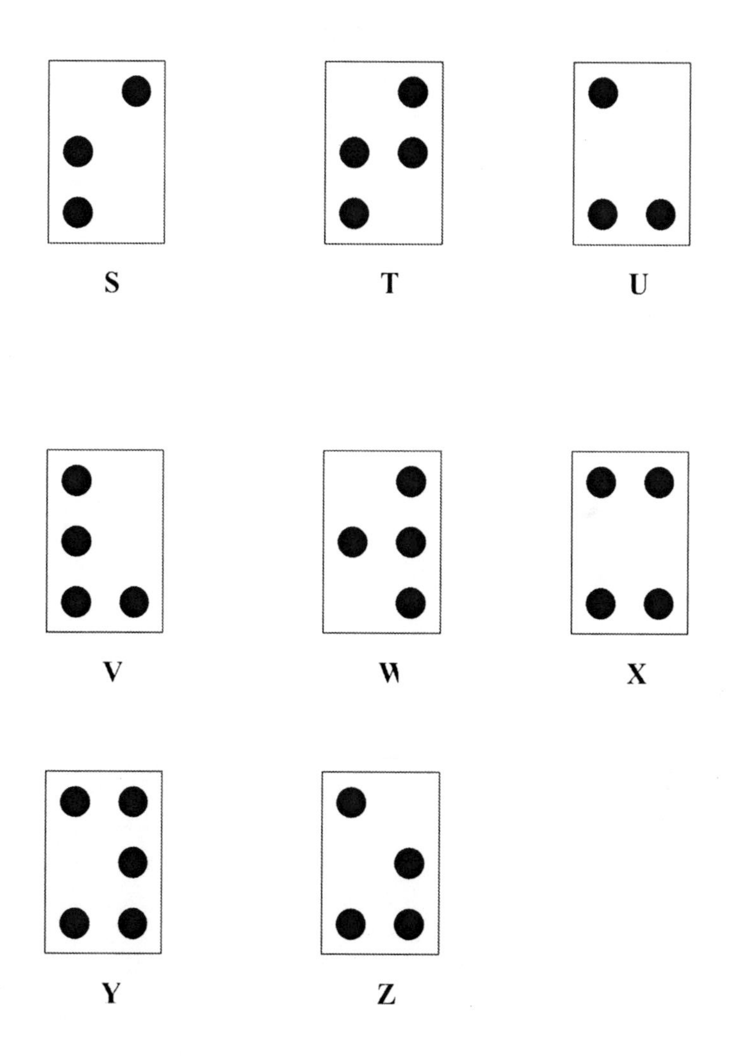
S
T
U
V
W
X
Y
Z

Dots and I are going to the zoo for a fun time. Why don't you come along and see if you can read the hidden Braille letters.

We're at the zoo now. Dots is so excited. "Slow down, Dots. We are running as quickly as we can."

Since Dots is crazy about the giraffes, I think that we'll go to see the giraffes first.

Dots and I both see a Braille letter from the spots on the giraffe. Can you name the letter?

Let's go see the leopards. Leopards have beautiful spots. I wonder if we will see any Braille letters on the leopard.

Dots is ready to see the snakes. He likes the snakes as long as they are inside of a glass aquarium.
Can you find the hidden Braille letter?
"Dots come out from behind the kindergarten child. The snakes are behind the glass. They won't get you."

Dots needs to look at something else besides the snakes. We are going to go and see the fish. The fish are located inside of a building. They will also be in glass aquariums.
Can you find another letter in Braille?

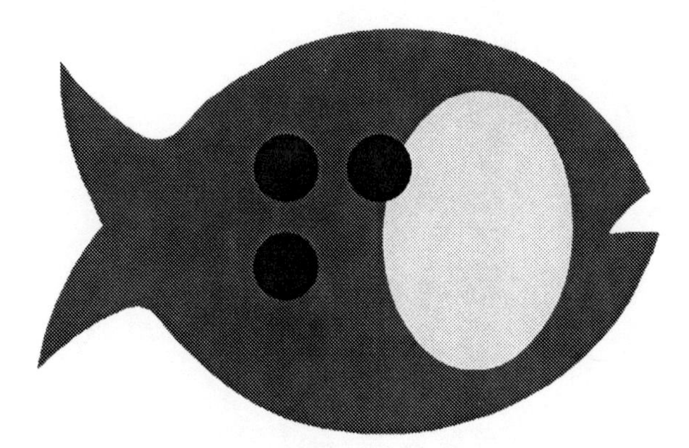

Dots and I can hear the monkeys playing. Let's go and see if we can see any Braille letters on the monkeys. "Stop eating the bananas, Dots. They are for the monkeys; not for a Braille cell."

"Hey, Dots. Look at that little boy laughing at the monkeys. Can you 'spot' another Braille letter? Haha. Get it, Dots. I said, 'spot'. Never mind, Dots."

There's another neat-o animal. It's a dolphin. The dolphin is really fun to watch. I think I see a letter on the dolphin. Do you know what it is?

Dots and I are getting hungry. I love to eat all of the great food at the zoo. Dots is buying his food now. I better get in line before the food is all gone. While we are eating, look for the Braille letter hidden on the hotdog. Can you find the letter?

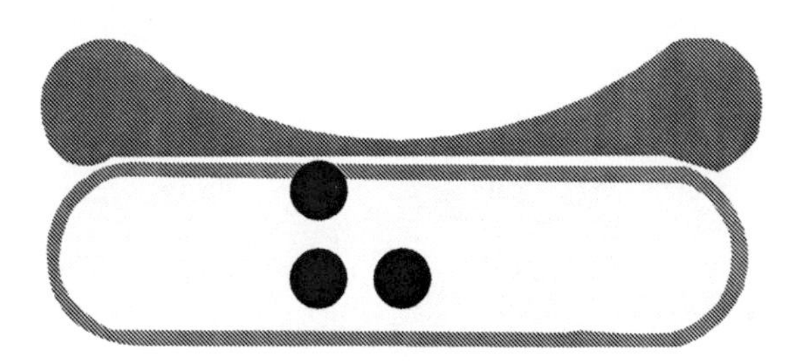

"Okay, Dots. I'll get a soda for you to drink, but only if the children can find the next hidden letter."

"Look over there, Dots. I hear a frog croaking in the pond where the lily pads are. The frog has a secret message written above him. Do you think the children can read the message?" Try to read the secret message using your Braille alphabet.

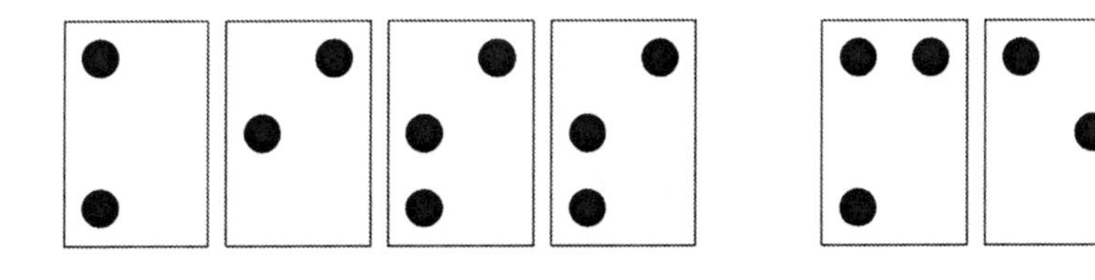

Dots is blushing, so we better move on and see other fun animals at the zoo. "Wow, Dots. Look at the beautiful peacock. I think that he is trying to tell us something." Can you read the message under the peacock?

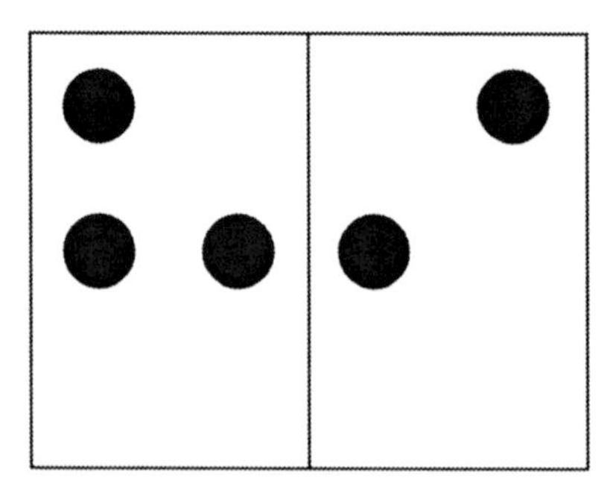

"Dots, our animal friends are really friendly. I see the Children's Petting Zoo up ahead. I want to meet some of our smaller animal friends. Let's buy some food for the animals so that we can feed them." Look and read the Braille letter if you can.

Everybody is doing an excellent job. Reading Braille is really fun and not hard if you keep learning the letters in Braille.

I hear a loud roar. It's the elephant and I see another Braille letter. I wonder what it is.

"Stop burying your head in the sand, Dots. The elephant will not hurt you or are you trying to be like the ostrich that is across the fence from the elephant?"

"Dust yourself off, Dots. It is time to move on and see more beautiful animals."
Up ahead there is a really pretty animal but he sounds scary. Good thing he is inside of a cage. Stay back from the cage and read the Braille letter.

Wow! I am having such a great time at the zoo. Let's go and ride the tram and see the entire zoo at one time. "It is okay, Dots. It travels a little high, but not as high as the roller coaster ride that made you cry. Sorry Dots, I shouldn't have brought that up again."

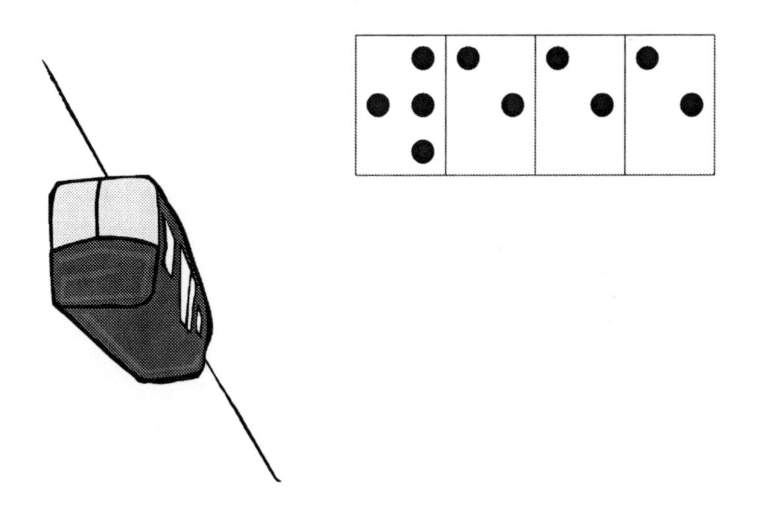

I can see so many animals, flowers and plants from up here. The tram is really fun to ride and you really get to see the animals well.

Dots is hungry again, so I guess we'll stop and get some ice cream. I love the ice cream covered with sprinkles and dots.

We haven't seen the polar bears or the gorillas, yet. Let's go and visit their habitats.

"Oh, sorry, Dots. A habitat means that the animals are in their natural environment. I bet the polar bears are in a nice and cool environment while the gorillas are in a jungle area with a lot of trees. Let's stop talking and get moving so that we can see these interesting animals."

There are the polar bears. Their habitat is nice and cool. It is so hot outside; I wish that I could go swimming in the pool but without the polar bears.

"Get ready, Dots. The gorillas can be a little scary but they are fascinating animals."

"Dots, where did you go? Come down out of the tree. I told you that he wouldn't get you. Now let's move on and go see the birds. Look at the red one."

What a fun day! It's time to leave the zoo and go back to school so that we can help our friends read more books in Braille.

Children without sight read Braille by touching the Braille with their fingertips. They are really smart to read the Braille by touch only.

Dots and I would like to give children more information about people who cannot see on the next few pages.

I hope that you had as much fun at the zoo as Dots and I did.

"Dottie and Dots See Animal Spots"

Dots and I went to the zoo,
To visit the animals there.
We were very surprised to see
That Braille dots were everywhere!

On animal tails and animal legs,
And even on animal faces,
Braille letters started appearing
In some of the strangest places.

The leaves on the trees were displaying
All kinds of letters and words.
We even saw some presented
On the wings of bats and birds.

The funny little monkeys in cages
All laughed as they twisted and turned.
They liked showing off to Dots and me
Some of the letters they'd learned.

All of the animals had letters ...
The fish, the tiger, the bear ...
The ostrich, the peacock, the leopard ...
Braille dots were everywhere!

When we left the zoo that day,
We spoke of the letters we'd found.
Now, Braille dots are waiting for you ...
Just stop and look all around!!

Jamille Smith 2007

TIPS FOR SIGHTED PEOPLE WHO KNOW A VIP (VISUALLY IMPAIRED PERSON)

Approach someone who cannot see with a friendly hello and tell them who you are. Do not ask them to guess who you are. This makes the person with a visual impairment uncomfortable because he may not recognize your voice.

Do not startle a person who has a visual impairment by grabbing their hand or arm. Talk to them first. Always ask their permission before you touch them, so that you do not startle them.

Allow the VIP to be as independent as possible but assist them when they need or ask for help.

Treat the VIP like you do everyone else with needed accommodations.